Brittany Wigfield
Illustrations by: Windel Eborlas

ISBN: Softcover 978-1-5144-5451-0
EBook 978-1-5144-5450-3

Print information available on the last page

Rev. date: 01/28/2016

To order additional copies of this book, contact:
Xlibris
1-888-795-4274
www.Xlibris.com
Orders@Xlibris.com

ACKNOWLEDGEMENTS

Thank you to my longtime friend Chloe for going over numerous versions of this story and for being my personal expert on all things children's books.

To my mom and dad who inspired and jumpstarted me on this process, thank you for believing in my vision and helping me share it with the world.

Thank you to my husband, Mark, for your unwavering encouragement and for being my biggest supporter.

Thank you to Tiffany McAvoy of Photography by Tiffany for permission to use your image "My Monty" and to Josh Kryzwonos for permission to use your image "Toby."

To my coworkers at WETRA, thank you first of all for all that you do for our riders and equine therapists. You make a difference in the lives of so many people each and every day, and inspire me with your dedication, passion, and commitment to therapeutic riding. Secondly, thank you to Becky, Paige, Sydney, and Jen for your creative contributions to this story.

Finally, thank you to Amanda and her family for allowing me to use her as my inspiration for this story.

DEDICATION

This book is dedicated to Amanda. Your enthusiasm for each and every day inspires me, and I am so happy to have had the opportunity to teach you riding lessons. I love your strength, your determination, your affinity for unicorns, and your love of the colour purple. Thank you for being a light to others, and for showing the world what all you can do.

SCHOOL

Amanda is different.
Her friends at school know.
She tries to move fast,
But can only move slow.
Her legs and her arms
Try to move just like theirs,
But they just aren't as strong,
So she needs a wheelchair.
When they run around,
She pushes and rolls.
She wants to play soccer,
She wants to score goals.
But the grass is too rough,
And her friends are too fast,
And Amanda just feels
Like she's always in last.

Amanda has dystonia,
A medical condition.
She tries to move her muscles,
But they just don't listen.
Sometimes they feel tight,
Like she's frozen in place.
Sometimes they feel loose,
And all over the place.
She can't tie her shoes,
She can't hold a fork.
Her class laughs and points.
They call her a dork.
But Amanda won't listen.
She's busy inside
Thinking of tonight,
When she's going to ride!

Well, maybe there's lots
That Amanda can't do.
But there is something special
She can do just like you.
Once every week,
she can go for a ride,
And forget about all
of the tears that she's cried.
Because Toby, her horse,
Is her friend 'til the end.
His love and his strength
He will always extend.
No matter her difference,
her wheelchair, her name,
Riding is something
She does just the same.

She pushes and rolls
Into the barn doors.
She's greeted by smiles
and then by her horse.
Toby is ready,
And he understands
That sometimes she struggles
With her legs and her hands.
But Toby just nickers
And bobs his head.
He's happy to see her.
"Hi Toby!" She says.
And she takes her time
Rolling up to his side,
But he just waits patiently,
For her to come ride.

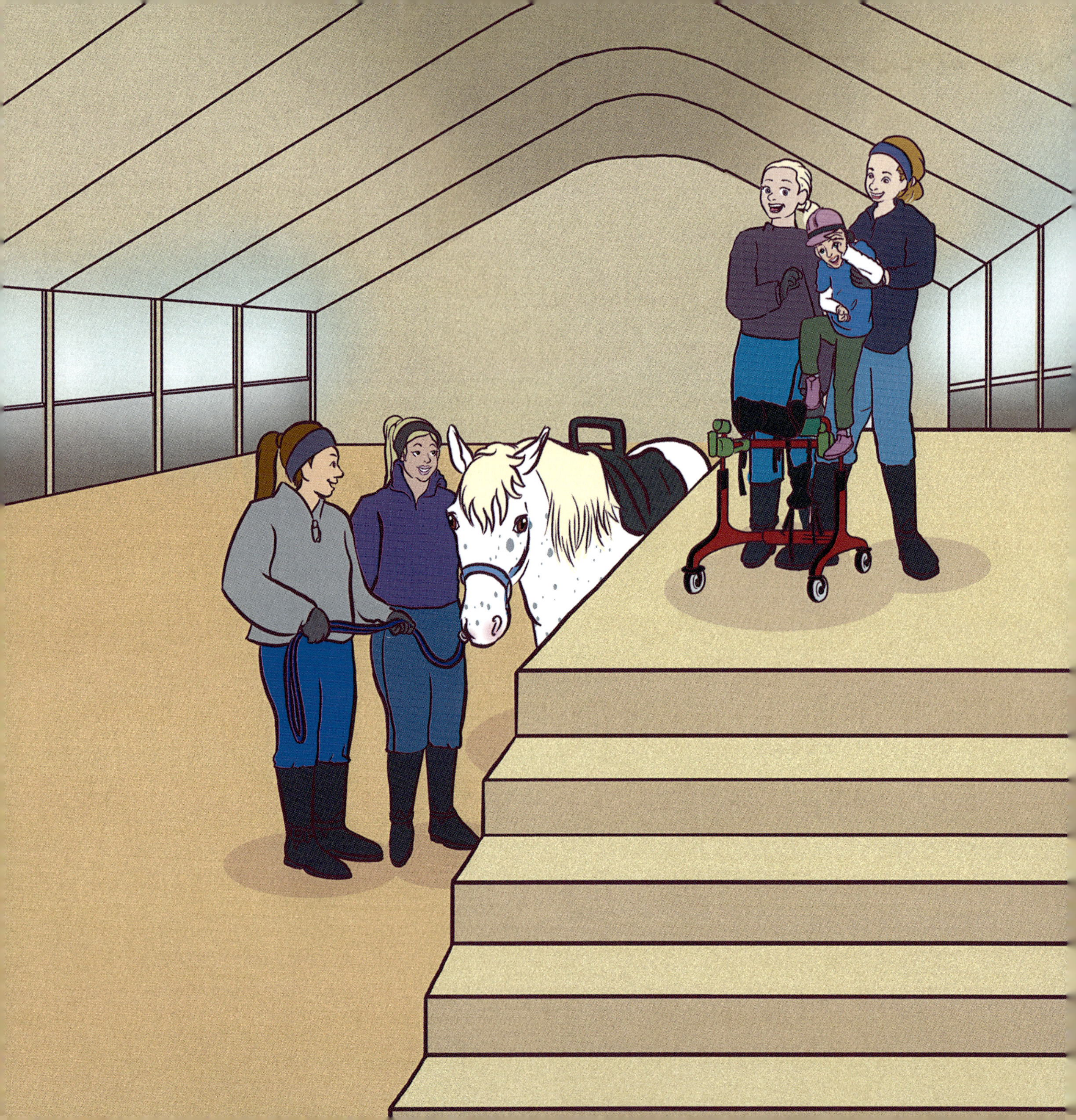

Amanda rolls onto
A ramp way up high,
And Toby stands still,
Just waiting beside.
The teachers lift her
On Toby's back,
And Amanda grabs hold
Of her special tack.
Her tack is her saddle,
A special type.
It has great big handles
For her to hold tight.
She runs her fingers
Through Toby's mane
And is happy that she
Can do something the same.

Her lesson begins
And Amanda sits tall.
She isn't afraid
That maybe she'll fall.
For Toby is steady,
and kind, and strong.
With him, Amanda feels
She can belong.
Because Toby, her horse,
Is her friend 'til the end.
His love and his strength
He will always extend.
No matter her difference,
her wheelchair, her name,
Riding is something
She does just the same.
She rides him in circles,
And squiggles and squares.
On Toby she feels
She can walk anywhere.
She does not have to worry
About grass or stones,
Toby can take her
Where she wants to go.

Amanda can steer him
And weave through the poles.
She can throw a basketball
And now score a goal.
Amanda can keep up
With all of her friends.
She feels like she's flying,
And starts to pretend.
As the lesson goes on,
Amanda's muscles get strong.
She's been working
To strengthen them all along.
There once was a time,
When they were so lax
She'd be laying down
On Toby's back.

With Toby,
Amanda can do what she can't
When she's on her own
Or at school with her friends.
Her lessons are special,
She feels the same.
Because of a horse,
And Toby's his name.
When her lesson is done,
Amanda gets down.
Back in her wheelchair,
She pushes around.
Before she leaves,
Toby nickers goodbye,
And Amanda knows
That she'll be alright.
Because Toby, her horse,
Is her friend 'til the end.
His love and his strength
He will always extend.
No matter her difference,
her wheelchair, her name,
Riding is something
She does just the same.

Bb
BALL
Cc
CAT
Dd
DOG
Ee
ELEPHANT
Ff
FISH
Gg
GRAPES
Hh
HEN
Ii
ICE CREAM
Jj
JUG
Kk
KITE
Ll
LION
Mm
MONKEY

The next day at school,
It's show and tell,
And Amanda has something
That she thinks is swell.
Tucked deep inside
Of her purple knapsack,
Is a picture of her
Riding on Toby's back.
She tells her whole class
Of the things she can do,
They listen in awe.
None of them knew!

Amanda looks different
than the rest of the group,
But her wheelchair is only
A tool she must use.
It does not mean she's odd,
or different, or weird.
It does not mean that she
Is someone to be feared.
The class learned Amanda
Can still come play games.
They learned there is lots
That she can do the same.

About Amanda:

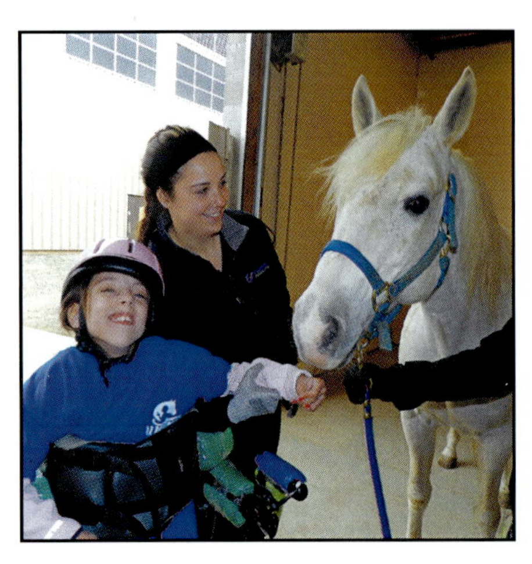

Amanda is 10 years old and in grade 5. She loves unicorns, dogs, and stuffed animals. Every week, Amanda enjoys coming to her therapeutic riding lessons with her twin brother, Matthew. After years of riding, she has had the opportunity to partner with many different horses at WETRA during her sessions including Sunny, Wendy, Simon, and Toby. Amanda has worked hard to share about therapeutic riding at school, and is happy to have many friends in her class who are kind, patient, and good at treating her just the same as anyone else. Her biggest goal is to travel to Hawaii to lay on the beach and swim with dolphins.

You can check out Amanda in action at her riding lessons by visiting https://www.youtube.com/watch?v=G1KGu_fSXZQ or by typing in “WETRA: Therapeutic Riding Benefits Everyone” in your YouTube search bar. Amanda stars in this video near the end after several other stories much like hers are shared and celebrated.

About WETRA:

Windsor-Essex Therapeutic Riding Association, or WETRA, is a therapeutic riding centre located in Essex, Ontario that is always seeking volunteers, donors, and sponsors. As a not-for-profit organization, the time and gifts of these people are the backbone of WETRA and all that it stands for. If you would like to make a donation, sponsor a horse, sponsor a rider, provide an item from WETRA's wish list, or become a volunteer, please visit www.wetra.ca and know that your help allows riders like Amanda to be able to come and receive therapeutic riding lessons that are truly life-changing.

About Toby:

Toby is a Welsh Pony and was born in 1997. He has served many clients as an equine therapist and is approaching his 8th year of service at WETRA after having retired from the show ring. He is a special horse who is exceptionally kind, patient, and understanding just like in this story.

Toby is unique because he lives and serves clients with only one eye after having the other eye removed in a surgery in 2015. He adjusted extremely well to having one eye, and is another example of how a different appearance does not mean a different personality, and that overcoming obstacles is easy with the right mindset. Toby sets a very high bar for other equine therapists to reach, and is one of the most reliable and faithful horses in the herd.

Toby and many of his friends are currently available for sponsorship at www.wetra.ca.

About Therapeutic Riding:

Therapeutic Riding, or Equine Therapy, is a growing trend in North America with centres located across both Canada and the United States. It allows for people with physical, mental, and emotional disabilities to have the opportunity to participate in therapy and treatment with a horse as an active participant in the session. The benefits have measurably shown improvements in areas such as balance, posture, muscle tone, coordination, confidence, concentration, strength, range of motion, fine and gross motor skills, and many others.

If you or someone you know may be a candidate for therapeutic riding centres, please research a centre near you for more information and to ensure you are a good fit for their programs.

Therapeutic Riding centres also rely on the contributions of countless volunteers who help facilitate riding lessons and care for the horses. Please contact a centre near you to see how you can get involved in this rewarding experience.

Edwards Brothers Malloy
Oxnard, CA USA
February 24, 2016